SIMON SPOTLIGHT & NICKELODEON PRESENT:

GO DIEGO GO!

· EXTREME RESCUE · MVFOL

CROCODILE MISSION

ERICA DAVID
writer

WARNER MCGEE
artist

LAURA LYN DISIENA
designer

SIOBHAN CIMINERA
editor

WENDY RUBIN
managing editor

D0515236

SIMON SPOTLIGHT/NICKELODEON NEW YORK LONDON TORONTO SYDNEY

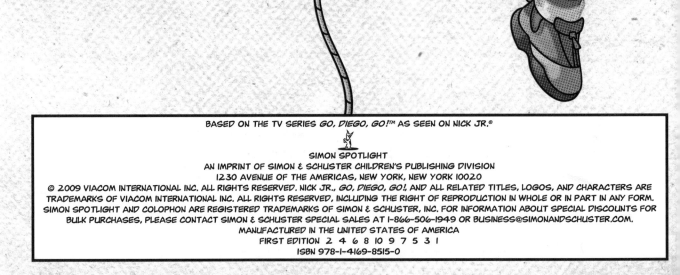

BASED ON THE TV SERIES *GO, DIEGO, GO!*™ AS SEEN ON NICK JR.®

SIMON SPOTLIGHT
AN IMPRINT OF SIMON & SCHUSTER CHILDREN'S PUBLISHING DIVISION
1230 AVENUE OF THE AMERICAS, NEW YORK, NEW YORK 10020
© 2009 VIACOM INTERNATIONAL INC. ALL RIGHTS RESERVED. NICK JR., *GO, DIEGO, GO!*, AND ALL RELATED TITLES, LOGOS, AND CHARACTERS ARE
TRADEMARKS OF VIACOM INTERNATIONAL INC. ALL RIGHTS RESERVED, INCLUDING THE RIGHT OF REPRODUCTION IN WHOLE OR IN PART IN ANY FORM.
SIMON SPOTLIGHT AND COLOPHON ARE REGISTERED TRADEMARKS OF SIMON & SCHUSTER, INC. FOR INFORMATION ABOUT SPECIAL DISCOUNTS FOR
BULK PURCHASES, PLEASE CONTACT SIMON & SCHUSTER SPECIAL SALES AT 1-866-506-1949 OR BUSINESS@SIMONANDSCHUSTER.COM.
MANUFACTURED IN THE UNITED STATES OF AMERICA
FIRST EDITION 2 4 6 8 10 9 7 5 3 1
ISBN 978-1-4169-8515-0

DIEGO WALKED DEEPER INTO THE SWAMP. HE CAREFULLY PICKED HIS WAY THROUGH THE BRANCHES AND VINES THAT BLOCKED HIS PATH. AFTER A WHILE HE FOUND HIMSELF WALKING DOWN A STEEP SLOPE.

WITHIN MINUTES THE SKY GREW DARK AND IT STARTED TO RAIN.

THE GROUND IS GETTING REALLY MUDDY. I'D BETTER BE CAREFUL!

THE RAIN POURED DOWN FROM THE DARK CLOUDS OVERHEAD. DIEGO HEARD A RUMBLING NOISE THAT SOUNDED LIKE THUNDER. BUT WHEN HE LOOKED BEHIND HIM, HE REALIZED IT WASN'T THUNDER AT ALL.

IT'S A MUDSLIDE!

THE WALL OF MUD OOZED DOWN THE SLOPE AFTER DIEGO!

DIEGO SWUNG LIKE A MONKEY FROM ONE VINE TO THE NEXT. WHAT A SPEEDY WAY TO TRAVEL!

IF WE STAND VERY STILL AND LISTEN CAREFULLY, MAYBE YOU CAN HEAR YOUR FAMILY AT THEIR NEW HOME.
LET'S TRY IT!